Blue

Sarah Christou

faber

Once, I had a secret that no one could see...

I thought of it as blue.

It made me feel
nervous on buses

and shy in
playgrounds,

and too worried to dance at parties.

In fact, it made me
worry about everything.

If I tried very hard,

sometimes

I could pretend it wasn't there.

But mostly, I couldn't.

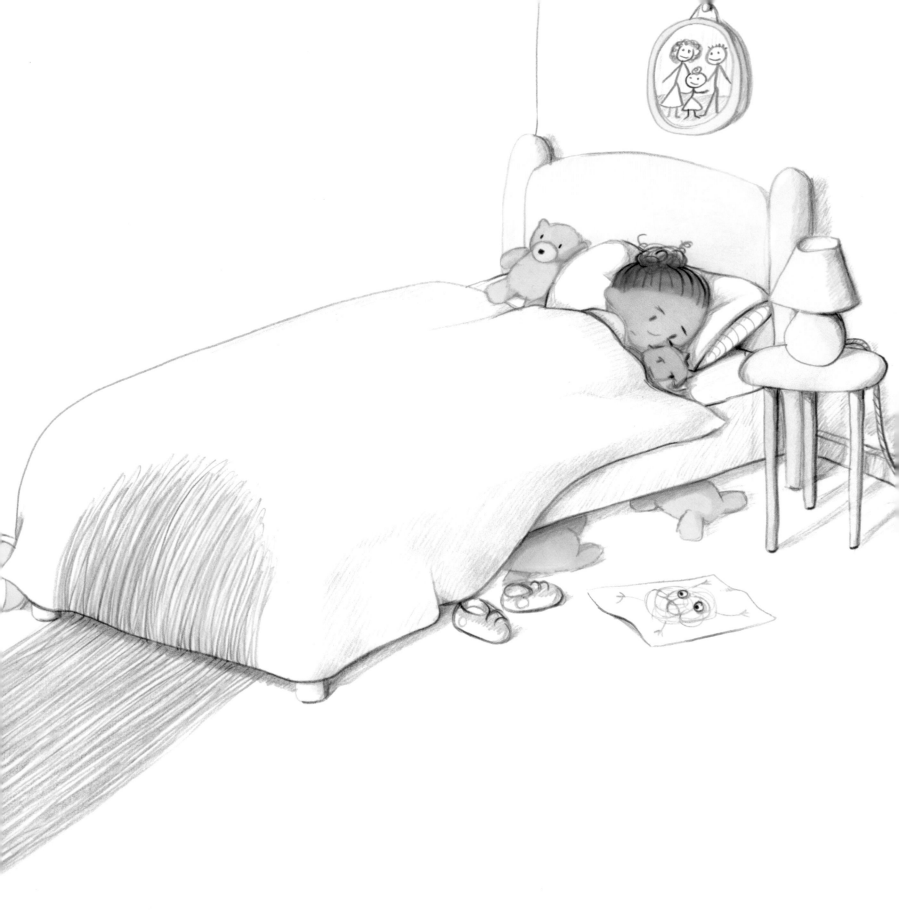

Then, on one
very blue day . . .

I told my friend,

and the next day,
I told another.

And suddenly, I knew
what I should have
known before . . .

I don't have to feel
sad things on my own.

(And neither do you.)

And it's okay
to talk about it

at school,

at home,

or even...

at the hairdresser's!

Or at night when I feel most alone.

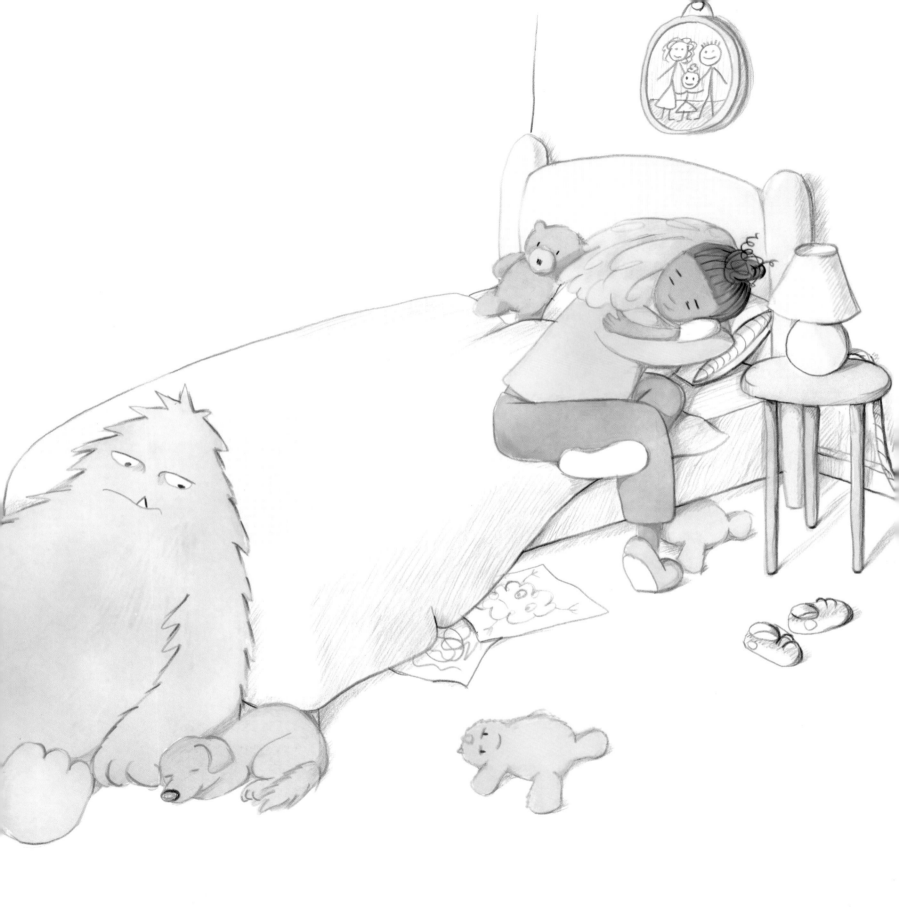

Because blue
is just a
colour...

in the rainbow of me.

For little Mark and Sarah

First published in the UK in 2023
First published in the US in 2023
by Faber and Faber Limited
Bloomsbury House,
74–77 Great Russell Street,
London WC1B 3DA
faber.co.uk
Text and illustrations © Sarah Christou, 2023
Design by Faber
HB ISBN 978–0–571–37635–3
PB ISBN 978–0–571–37636–0
All rights reserved
Printed in India
2 4 6 8 10 9 7 5 3 1
The moral rights of Sarah Christou have been asserted
A CIP record for this book is available from the British Library

Faber has published children's books since 1929.
T. S. Eliot's *Old Possum's Book of Practical Cats* and
Ted Hughes' *The Iron Man* were amongst the first. Our
catalogue at the time said that 'it is by reading such
books that children learn the difference between the
shoddy and the genuine'. We still believe in the power
of reading to transform children's lives. All our books
are chosen with the express intention of growing a
love of reading, a thirst for knowledge and to cultivate
empathy. We pride ourselves on responsible editing.
Last but not least, we believe in kind and inclusive books
in which all children feel represented and important.